FRANK PERETTI

as Mr. Henry

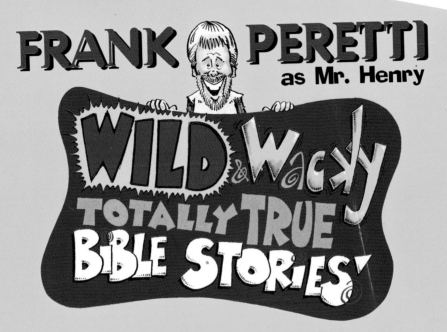

WILD & WACKY TOTALLY TRUE BIBLE STORIES

ALL ABOUT FAITH

Illustrated by Bill Ross

Tommy NELSON

www.tommynelson.com

A Division of Thomas Nelson, Inc.
www.ThomasNelson.com

Library of Congress Cataloging-in-Publication Data

Peretti, Frank E.
    Wild & wacky totally true Bible stories : all about faith / Frank Peretti, as Mr. Henry ;
illustrated by Bill Ross.
        p. cm.
    Summary: Humorous retellings of three Bible stories about faith, each with an introduction and follow-up by "Mr. Henry," who relates the experiences of Noah, Moses, and Daniel to modern life.
    ISBN 1-4003-0014-2 (hc)
    1. Faith—Biblical teaching—Juvenile literature. 2. Bible stories, English. [1. Faith. 2. Bible stories—O.T. 3. Noah (Biblical figure) 4. Moses (Biblical leader) 5. Daniel (Biblical character)] I. Title: Wild and wacky totally true Bible stories. II. Ross, Bill, 1956–   ill. III. Title.

BS1199.F3 P47 2002
221.9'505—dc21

                                                                    2002033681

Printed in Colombia

03 04 05 06 07 QWQ 9 8 7 6 5 4 3 2 1

A WAY BIG BOAT

ALL ABOUT FAITH

Whack! Oh, hi. I'm Mr. Henry. Ouch.

I bonk my head on that board all the time. When we built this workshop, my builder said to never, ever remove this piece of wood, or the whole roof would cave in! But it sure hurts when I smack my head on this thing.

It should say, "Watch out!"

Instead it says, "**NOAH's BIG BOAT.**"

Let me tell you the story of Noah and his boat . . .

There once lived a man named Noah, one of the most faithful guys in the whole Bible. One bright day, as Noah watered his garden, he heard a voice calling, "Noooaaahhhh! Noah!"

"Is that You, God?" Noah asked.

"Yes. I must tell you that I plan to destroy the earth and every living creature. I am sad that I ever made all these things. The people are mean and **wicked** except for you and your family. So I will make it rain until the whole earth floods. To save your family, you will need a really big boat."

God told Noah how big to build his boat—450 feet long,
75 feet wide, and 45 feet high. Way **BIG!** Noah's
neighbors watched, amused, as he worked in his front yard.

Like all the other people, these neighbors were not nice at
all. That's why God planned to give the whole world a good,
cleansing bath. Even though his neighbors made fun of him,
Noah's faith in God gave him the strength to obey.

"Noah's gone nutso," one neighbor scoffed.

"Yep. He's bonkers," said another.

God sent two of every animal—one female and one male—to Noah's boat. "Step right up," Noah yelled to the zebras. "Don't be shy," he called to the tigers.

Noah welcomed the dogs, cats, alligators, gerbils, koala bears, and all the other animals. Then Noah gathered his family.

"Everyone, it's time to go on our family cruise."

"With all these animals?" Noah's son Ham whined. "I'm allergic to zebras."

"*Achoo!* And to monkeys," added Ham's wife.

Just then, raindrops started to fall. Forgetting all about their allergies, Noah's family leaped into the boat.

The rain **POUNDED** down as Noah's neighbors pounded on the door of the boat, begging Noah to take them, too.

"Noah! We want to go with you!"

"Noah, open the door!"

"Noah, let us in!"

But Noah couldn't let them in. God had sealed the door.

Just as God had declared, it poured for forty long days and even longer nights. They seemed especially long for Noah and his family, who felt like chickens cooped up with the chickens.

"Hey, Papa! I thought you said this family vacation would be like a cruise," moaned Noah's son Japheth.

"Yeah!" chimed in Noah's other son, Shem. "What happened to five-course meals? I'm sharing a stateroom with a giraffe."

"Boys!" Noah yelled. "Stop your whining. Our faithful God is taking good care of us. Ever heard of being thankful?"

Finally the rain stopped. But water still covered the earth for a long time.

Then one day, Noah sent a dove out to search for land. That evening, when the dove flew back carrying a fresh **olive** leaf in its mouth, Noah knew the bird had found a dry patch of land.

Two months later, God told Noah that everyone could get out of the boat.

Noah's family ran around on the bright-green grass, playing tag. As he watched the animals chase each other, Noah heard a voice.

"Noooaaahhhh! Noah!"

"Yes, God," he answered, as a moose licked his nose.

"I promise that I will never again send a flood to destroy the earth."

Noah smiled, and God sealed His promise with a RAINBOW.

God always does what He says He will. God promised Noah
He would take care of his family. Sure enough, God delivered.
   Do you have enough **faith** to obey God, even if He asks
you to do something that sounds weird? Even if people make
fun of you? Being faithful worked for Noah! It can work for
you, too!

Moses
6 WHINING & MOANING

ALL ABOUT FAITH

It seems like there's always something to clean up around here. I hate cleaning. First I have to put everything away, and then I have to wipe everything down, dust everything off, and sweep away all of the dirt.

Now, *who* left this old box of Manna Wafers on the mantel?

Wow. Listen to me. I'm complaining just like a bunch of "moan-heads" did way back in Moses' time. If they had just obeyed God without bellyaching, their lives might have been a lot easier.

One day, when Moses and the Israelites were backpacking to the Promised Land, God told Moses to meet Him on top of Mount Sinai. He wanted to give Moses some instructions He'd written on two **STONE** tablets.

Before Moses left, he gathered everyone together. "Okay, listen up," he said. "I'm going to be tied up in an important meeting with God. While I'm gone, I'm leaving Aaron in charge!"

Imagine! A meeting with God. The people thought that was pretty cool—at least, for a while.

But soon they began to complain. "When's Moses coming back?" they whined to Aaron. "He's been gone forever! Make us some nice shiny gods so we can worship them and have fun! Pleeease!"

Aaron *should* have said, "Are you nuts? No way!" But he didn't.

Instead, Aaron said, "Okay, travelers, wanderers, and tagalongs, lend me your earrings!"

They melted the earrings and made a golden calf. Then came PARTY time . . .

Meanwhile, God told Moses what was happening below.
Moses stormed down that mountainside. When he saw the
golden calf, he practically had a cow. "You want to party?!"
he yelled. "We're going to make a pot of Golden Calf Soup—
and you're going to eat every drop!"

Then Moses made the people start their journey again.
And even though they'd been bad, God provided them with
good food. They called it **"MANNA."** But the people got
tired of manna.

Soon *everyone* began to yell: "Meat! Meat! We want meat!"
God grew very angry, and Moses got upset too.

"Lord," Moses cried, "why am I in charge of these moan-
heads? I'm not their daddy or their nanny. Where am I
supposed to get meat for all these people?"

Well, God came through again. He gave the people meat.
In fact, He gave them a lot of meat! So much that the people
actually got sick of it—and sick to their stomachs. Did
they learn a lesson from this? Nope!

Even though God met their needs, the people started to *complain again*.

One girl said, "I hate marching in the desert. Sand gets all in my shoes."

Someone else cried, "Sand and manna. Manna and sand. We've got no bread. We've got no water. We've got no air conditioners!"

Then a little boy yelled out, pointing, "Hey! What are all those squiggly things?"

"Snakes!"

Hundreds of snakes slithered toward them. Snakes glided through the campsite and wriggled into tents. Some began to bite people. Lots of people got sick, and many of them died.

"Please, Moses," others begged. "Ask God to get rid of these snakes! They scare us!"

So Moses prayed, but God didn't send away the snakes. Instead, He told Moses to make a bronze snake and put it on a pole.

"Okay, people," Moses said. "I'm going to put this snake where everyone can see it. If you get bitten, just *look* at the bronze snake, and you won't die."

Do you think that put an end to all the complaining? Well, can snakes fly? Ha!

The moan-heads hadn't obeyed God in the beginning, and they didn't obey Him later, either. They could have reached the Promised Land in just a few weeks, but because of their disobedience, it took them **forty** years!

If we have faith in God, we will do what He asks of us. I think I'll finish my cleaning without being a moan-head, and I can start by "polishing off" this box of Manna Wafers.

ALL ABOUT **FAITH**

It must be here somewhere. If only I could find it . . . It's not in the breadbox. It's not under the table. Ah yes! Now I remember! It's in the oven. I'm sure of it.

I must have left it there when I baked rock cookies. Or was that the day I made rock candy? Never mind, here it is—the rock that kept Daniel from escaping a scary lions' den.

But Daniel knew that God would take care of him. When Daniel was trappEd in that lions' den, God saved him! Let me tell you the story.

There once lived a king with a really looong name: Nebuchadnezzar. Let's just call him King Nebbie. He felt crabbier than a crab cake because he had so many **bad** dreams. But a wise man named Daniel came to help him.

King Nebbie asked, "Can you tell me what my dreams mean?"

Daniel answered, "I can't, but God can."

The king told Daniel that in one dream, a **BIG** tree was going to get chopped down.

With God's help, Daniel explained the king's dream. "This dream is about you," said Daniel. "Just like the tree, you're big and strong. But you're going to get cut down."

Daniel said that God was unhappy because King Nebbie tried to turn people away from God. So the dream meant the king wouldn't be king much longer. And sure enough—chop-chop—King Nebbie soon became plain old Nebbie.

Later on, Daniel worked for another king named Darius—a much shorter name. He was a nicer king, too. He liked Daniel. But others who worked for King Darius were jealous of Daniel, and they wanted to get him in trouble.

They made a plan. One worker said to the king, "You should make a law that for one month, no one can pray to anyone but you. You. You. You." That sounded like a good idea to Darius.

But all the workers knew that Daniel prayed to God three times a day. **One. Two. Three.**

And Daniel kept praying to God even after the new law passed. So the workers' mean trick worked: Daniel got in trouble with a capital *T*.

When he made his new law, King Darius didn't realize he would have to punish his good friend. *What was I thinking?* he asked himself. He tried to figure out a way to save Daniel. But the law couldn't be changed. Sadly, the king ordered his guards: "Throw Daniel into the lions' den."

Big, hungry lions were inside, waiting for their next meal.

"Daniel," said the king, "you broke a law when you prayed to God. I have to punish you. I'm sorry, and I hope your God saves you."

The king's guards threw Daniel into the lions' den. Then they pushed a huge rock in front of its opening to keep Daniel inside.

The lions **g-r-r-r-rowled** and looked at Daniel like he was lunchmeat. Daniel prayed, "God, help me. I'm scared. These lions are bigger than me."

King Darius couldn't sleep at all that night. But in the lions' den, an ANGEL had appeared. The angel held the big jaws of the lions closed—and kept them shut tight all night—so they couldn't hurt Daniel.

The next morning, the king rushed to the den. "Guards, move that stone!" he demanded. "Daniel! Are you okay? Did your God save you from the lions?"

"Yes, I'm here!" Daniel answered.

Happy, the king demanded: "Get Daniel out of that den right now!"

So, they freed Daniel.

He hadn't been hurt at all because he had faith in God's protection.

But things didn't work out too well for the workers who had tricked King Darius. He threw *them* into the lions' den. Now who felt like lunchmeat?

Did you know that God is always with you? Even when you're scared, God is there. He is! God is bigger than any grouchy king. He's bigger than mean, hungry lions. He's **HUGE!**

He can help when you get in trouble, just like He helped Daniel. Just have faith in Him, and pray when you're scared. God is stronger than the biggest rock. He'll take care of you.